Christmas Crackers

Follow the Glitter Girls' latest adventures!
Collect the other fantastic books in the series:

Caroline Plaisted

Christmas Crackers

SCHOLASTIC

Scholastic Children's Books,
Commonwealth House, 1-19 New Oxford Street,
London WC1A 1NU, UK
a division of Scholastic Ltd

London ~ New York ~ Toronto ~ Sydney ~ Auckland
Mexico City ~ New Delhi ~ Hong Kong

Published by Scholastic Ltd, 2002

ISBN 0 439 98125 5

Typeset by Falcon Oast Graphic Art Ltd
Printed and bound in Denmark by Nørhaven Paperback, Viborg

2 4 6 8 10 9 7 5 3

Chapter 1

It was a cold day in November and the Glitter Girls had just finished school for the day.

"Come on!" Charly urged as they raced towards Mrs Giles's car. "It's freezing out here!"

"Yes!" agreed Meg. "Hurry up and get in."

She opened the car door and the other Glitter Girls hopped in.

"Hello, girls." Mrs Giles smiled at them. "Good day?"

"Pretty cool," Flo said. "We had art today and started doing stuff for Christmas."

"I love Christmas," Zoe exclaimed. "It's just the best time of year, isn't it?"

"All those presents!" Hannah agreed.

"And all that delicious food, too!" Charly

added, pushing her pink glasses back up on her nose.

"You know," Mrs Giles said, as she pulled out into the traffic. "I was thinking about Christmas today at work, as well."

Hannah's mum worked at the local theatre where she made costumes for all of the productions. She was brilliant at sewing and had made the Glitter Girls' special denim jackets that they all loved wearing whenever they could.

"Why was that, Mum?" Hannah asked as she plaited a section of her long red hair.

"Well, we were talking about the Christmas pantomime. . ." Mrs Giles explained.

"Oh, last year's was brilliant!" Charly said, excitedly. *"Peter Pan!"*

"With Will and Gareth from *Pop Idol!*" Flo sighed.

"Fantastic!" the others agreed.

At the pantomime last Christmas, Mrs Giles

had arranged for the Glitter Girls to have special seats at the theatre. They'd gone to see the performance and then, as an extra-special treat, Hannah's mum had arranged for them to go back stage to meet all the stars! Martine McCutcheon had been Peter Pan!

"What's the pantomime going to be this Christmas, Mum?" Hannah asked.

"*Cinderella*," Mrs Giles explained.

"And who's going to be in it?" Flo wanted to know.

"Well, Cat Deeley's going to be Cinderella, and Ant and Dec are going to be the Ugly Sisters!" Mrs Giles said.

"Wow!" exclaimed Zoe.

"We've absolutely got to go now!" agreed Hannah.

"Who's going to be Buttons?" Charly asked.

"Not sure about that at the moment," Mrs Giles replied. "They're still holding auditions to find the best people."

"It sounds great!" Flo said, smiling, "Can you get us tickets? Please, Mrs Giles?"

"Yes – *please!*" all the other Glitter Girls joined in.

"Well, actually. . ." Mrs Giles said, grinning as she pulled up outside her house and switched off the car's engine. "Actually, I didn't think you'd want to just go and see the pantomime this year."

"What?" Hannah exclaimed. "Of course we want to go to the pantomime! It's going to be great!"

"Yes!" said Flo and Meg together.

"So you're not too grown-up for the pantomime then?" Hannah's mum teased.

"Course not!" said Zoe.

"Well, that's good," said Mrs Giles, turning round in her seat to look at all of the Glitter Girls together, "because the director of the pantomime needs some extras to help in the show – to be mice, in fact," she explained.

"Where's he going to find the extras?" Meg asked.

"That's just what I was going to tell you." Mrs Giles grinned. "He's going to hold auditions for the parts – there are ten of them – at the theatre this weekend."

"Wow!" Meg exclaimed. "Do you think he might want some children to do the parts?"

Mrs Giles laughed. "I think so!"

The Glitter Girls erupted in an explosion of excited giggles.

"Do you think we can audition?" Flo wondered.

"I'm sure my mum would let me if I ask her!" Charly cried.

"And mine!" added Zoe.

"It could be our next adventure!" concluded Meg, tucking a stray lock of her blonde curly hair behind her ear.

"Oh, Mum – can we?" Hannah begged.

"Shush, shush!" Mrs Giles waved her hands at

the Glitter Girls, trying to calm them down. "Actually – I've already spoken to your parents about this."

"And?" the girls all asked together.

"And they've said yes! You can come to the theatre on Saturday to audition for the parts," said Mrs Giles, smiling.

"Go Glitter!" the girls all screamed at once.

It looked as if another Glitter Girl adventure had begun!

Chapter 2

After eating their tea in record time, the Glitter Girls gathered together in Hannah's bedroom for one of their meetings.

"What should we practise?" Flo asked. "You know – for the audition?"

"What do you mean?" Zoe wondered, pulling up her shimmering pink socks. She wasn't really allowed to wear socks like that to school but, because it was so cold now, she had been wearing trousers to school and had managed to hide the socks under them!

"We need an audition piece, like Mum said," Hannah replied. "We need to have a routine or something for Saturday."

"Your mum said that they wanted people who

could dance as well as sing, didn't she?" Charly commented.

"That's true," Meg agreed. "So maybe they'll ask us to join in with some routines that they've organized – that include singing and dancing."

"Oh," sighed Flo. "I'm not sure I could manage something like that. I mean I can sing but I'm not so good at dancing."

"Course you can!" said Meg. "Remember that television series they had back in the summer? When all those people went along to audition for a part in a musical?"

"Yes!" said Charly, who wanted so much to be a television presenter one day. "It was great – why don't we put a piece together like they did?"

"Yeah, we need to work *something* out," Hannah said, flicking her hair back behind her shoulders. "We should have a routine put together just in case."

"OK," said Meg, pulling out her notebook and pen from her school bag. "So what should we do?"

"Well, we haven't got very long, have we?" Zoe moaned.

"No. . ." Charly agreed, sounding a bit dejected. "I mean how can we choreograph a new routine in only four days?"

"With difficulty!" exclaimed Hannah, who because she wanted to be a dancer, couldn't bear the thought of not getting a routine absolutely perfect.

The Glitter Girls looked around at each other, all hoping that one of them could come up with a solution to their problem. It was beginning to look as if their next adventure was doomed before it had even begun.

"*I* know!" said Meg excitedly.

"What?" the others all demanded.

"What about if we do a version of someone else's video routine?" Meg said.

"Of course!" Zoe cried. "Like S Club 7 or something!"

"Yes," agreed Flo.

Thankfully, Meg had found the answer to their problem and the Glitter Girls spent the next half an hour trying to decide which was their favourite video routine. In the end, they decided to go for one of S Club Juniors' latest top-ten hits because it had a really catchy tune with something for all of them to sing solo. It also had a cool dance routine that they already knew quite well.

"I've got a video of them from *Top of the Pops*," said Zoe. "You know, when they got to number two in the charts and went on to do it live?"

"Yes!" said Flo. "They were so cool!"

"*And* they were wearing their denim jackets!" Charly said.

"Like our Glitter Girl ones!" Hannah laughed.

"Sorted!" said Meg. "Shall we rehearse it tomorrow, after school?"

The others agreed.

"So what are we going to wear?" Flo wanted to know.

"Our jackets and jeans of course!" said Charly.

"We'd look good in those," Hannah agreed. "But we can't dance our best in jeans, can we?"

"No," Zoe said. "They'd be too tight!"

"How about our baggy combats?" Flo suggested.

"Sounds good to me," agreed Charly.

"OK," Meg said, scribbling all of this down. "Let's all wear something like that with a cool T-shirt under our jackets, and trainers."

"Go Glitter!" the others yelled in response.

★ ♥ ★ ♥ ★ ♥ ★

At school the next day, the Glitter Girls were keen to practise some of the S Club Juniors' routine. They even managed to sneak in a quick rehearsal in the playground at breaktime. Between them, they remembered most of the routine but Hannah had watched the video again the night before and helped everyone out.

"We're going to need to rehearse a lot," she said. "Especially if we're going to get this to look really good."

"No worries," said Meg, smiling confidently. "We'll do it!"

"Go Glitter!" the others agreed.

When the bell went, the girls rushed outside to meet Charly's mum, who took them back to the Fishers' house for tea. Lily, Charly's younger sister, was just as pleased as the Glitter Girls were about Saturday's audition.

"Go Glitter!" Lily shouted, waving her hands above her head in the car on the way home.

"Go Glitter!" the five best friends called back, giggling with Lily.

As soon as they arrived at Charly's house, the Glitter Girls raced upstairs to rehearse to a CD that Meg had brought with her.

Once they were in Charly's room, they moved furniture out of the way before putting the CD on to play. S Club Juniors were such good singers that the Glitter Girls found it infectious and tapped their feet ready to begin as the backing track started up.

"Five, six, seven, eight!" Hannah counted.

And their first rehearsal began. But after only a few steps, trouble began.

"Ouch!" squeaked Zoe, stubbing her toe on the end of Charly's bed.

"This is harder than I'd thought," sighed Meg, as she went over to stop the CD.

"It's not hard," moaned Hannah. "It's just that this room isn't big enough!"

"How can we rehearse properly in here?" Zoe said, still rubbing her sore toe.

"We can't!" said Charly. "Sorry. . ."

"It's not your fault," Flo said, hugging her friend. "It would be the same in all of our bedrooms, wouldn't it?"

"Yes," agreed Meg, and she fiddled with her favourite butterfly clip in her hair. "What are we going to do?"

The Glitter Girls thought for a moment.

"Got it!" Flo said, smiling. "Do you think we could rehearse in your garage, Zoe – like we did for the talent competition?"

"That's a great idea!" said Zoe. "I'm sure it'll be OK. I'll check with Dad tonight."

"If he says yes," Hannah said, smiling, "we could still squeeze in two more rehearsals before Saturday!"

Just then, Lily came in to Charly's room to tell them to come down for tea and the Glitter Girls raced downstairs and tucked into the spread of pizzas and sandwiches before them on the kitchen table.

"So how did your rehearsal go?" Mrs Fisher asked.

The Glitter Girls explained.

"Well – at least you've still got a few days to

perfect your routine," Mrs Fisher said. "And using Zoe's garage sounds like an excellent solution."

"I really hope we get parts in the pantomime!" Hannah sighed.

"It would be great if we could, wouldn't it?" Charly agreed.

The others nodded, still eating.

"I was organizing things for Christmas myself this morning – at Lily's nursery school," Mrs Fisher said. "We're going to run Santa's Grotto at the town's Christmas Bazaar this year!"

"Fantastic!" said Zoe.

"I love the Christmas Bazaar!" Flo said excitedly.

"Me too," said Meg. "We go every year!"

"So what do you have to do for the grotto, Mum?" Charly asked.

"Well, your dad's agreed to play the part of Father Christmas," Mrs Fisher explained. "And we need to organize some helpers to lead the little children into the grotto to meet Father Christmas and get their presents."

"Oh, can we help?" Flo cried.

"We could be the helpers!" exclaimed Zoe enthusiastically.

"Yes!" agreed Meg, Charly and Hannah.

Mrs Fisher smiled at the Glitter Girls around her kitchen table.

"I thought you'd never ask!" She laughed. "Of course you can help!"

"Brilliant!" said Hannah.

"Perfect!" said Zoe.

"It looks like this Christmas might be a busy one!" Flo said, grinning widely. "Go Glitter!"

Chapter 3

On Thursday and Friday evening, the Glitter Girls practised their routine in the garage at Zoe's house. They wanted to make sure that they were going to get everything just right for the audition on Saturday.

Now it was late on Friday, and they were preparing to run through the number for the last time.

"OK, everyone? Starting positions please!" Hannah pressed *play* on the CD player and quickly rushed to take her place.

The beat of the music pumped around the garage and the Glitter Girls could feel the excitement as they counted in to the start of their song and dance routine. Everything was going perfectly – they were almost at the end. It was the bit when they were all singing and dancing the same routine. Only Meg suddenly started to do a different step to everyone else and flung her arm out to one side, beginning to move round the others. Confused, the other girls thought they were going wrong and suddenly they were all going in different directions! Disaster! Meg had run into Zoe and Flo and the three of them came crashing to the ground.

"Oww!" yelled Zoe as the other two landed on top of her.

"Meg!" Flo cried.

"Oh no." Meg blushed. "I'm so sorry. Are you two OK?" She felt really bad about messing up the routine.

Hannah rushed over to switch off the music and then returned to join Charly who was helping the others back on to their feet.

"What on earth happened there?" Hannah demanded. "Didn't you count, Meg?"

"Of course I did!" Meg shouted, feeling cross and embarrassed. "I just got the steps wrong – OK? We can't all be great dancers like you, Hannah!"

Meg could feel tears pricking her eyes. She knew she shouldn't have shouted at Hannah but she was so upset at spoiling the routine. Immediately though, her friends realized how rotten she was feeling.

"I'm sorry, Meg," Hannah said. "I didn't mean to get at you."

"That's OK," Meg said, rearranging her ponytail, which had got messed up in the tumble. "You all right, Zoe?"

"I'll be fine," Zoe smiled back.

"Come on then," Hannah said. "Let's have another go. It'll be better this time, I'm sure."

Hannah ran through the step with Meg again and they all started at the beginning of the routine once more. Fortunately, this time it went perfectly and all of them, especially Meg, felt much happier with the result. As the music faded out on the track, Charly punched the air with her fist.

"Go Glitter!" she cried, feeling pleased with what they'd just achieved.

"Go Glitter!" her four friends replied.

★　♥　★　♥　★　♥　★

After they had tidied things away in the garage, the girls gathered in Zoe's kitchen to have a drink while they waited for their various parents to pick them up. Still feeling bad about making a mistake, and wanting to be as organized as ever, Meg took the opportunity to get her notebook out of her pocket and check a few things with the other Glitter Girls, in preparation for the audition the next day.

"OK," she said. "So we're meeting up at Hannah's house at about ten so that we can do our hair and stuff. Has everyone got what they need for that?"

The four others nodded their agreement.

"How are we going to wear our hair – just loose?" Zoe wondered.

"I think we should do some plaits and braids," Flo said.

"Yes," said Hannah. "It would be good to have it loose but if we braid up the front it will keep it out of our eyes when we're dancing."

"Good idea," said Charly, pulling the front of her own hair up and away from her face.

"OK, when we're dressed and stuff, Mrs Giles will take us to the theatre at about half-ten, ready for the audition at eleven!" Meg ticked things off on the list she had already written in her notebook the night before.

"I'm really looking forward to it," Charly said. "Do you think we'll get to see any of the stars tomorrow?"

"I doubt it," Flo sighed.

"No," Zoe agreed. "I shouldn't think they'll be around until the proper rehearsals start."

"You're probably right," Meg said, flipping her notebook shut. At the same time, the doorbell rang.

It was time for the Glitter Girls to go home and get a good night's sleep before the next day's excitement!

★ ♥ ★ ♥ ★ ♥ ★

Despite the butterflies in their tummies, the Glitter Girls managed to sleep quite well and they all woke up in the morning raring to go! As arranged, they met up at Hannah's, and immediately rushed to her bedroom to get ready.

"I brought some nail-art stuff," Charly explained, pulling lots of colourful nail polishes and decorations out of her backpack.

"Good idea!" Flo said.

"And I brought some hair accessories!" Zoe grinned.

It was just like the time the Glitter Girls had

run the Magical Makeovers stall at their school fête!

"Do you think we've got long enough?" Meg wondered, looking at her watch.

"We do if we all help each other and get going straight away!" Hannah said.

"Go Glitter!" the others agreed.

Meg, Hannah, Flo, Charly and Zoe immediately started to brush one another's hair. Then they busied themselves with threading in various beads and ribbons before taking it in turns to decorate each other's nails. Pretty soon they all looked fantastic.

"How do we look?" Hannah asked her friends.

"Like Glitter Girls!" Meg laughed.

"Or at least we will do when we've used this!" Zoe said, pulling a small tube from her bag.

"What's that?" Flo asked.

"Hey!" exclaimed Charly. "Isn't that the new body glitter that they sell at Girl's Dream?"

Girl's Dream was the Glitter Girls' favourite

shop. It sold everything – from pencils and toys to clothes and make-up – that the Glitter Girls could ever want.

"Come on – let's put a little bit on our cheeks!" Zoe suggested.

When the five of them were finished, they looked in the mirror that hung on the wall next to Hannah's bed. It was a tall mirror, framed with a gorgeous pink, fluffy feather boa! Hannah's mum had made it for her last year.

"Hey, wow!" Hannah cried. "Do you think the people at the audition will notice us?"

"I reckon!" Flo agreed.

Just then there was a knock at the door.

"Yes?" Hannah called.

"We have to leave in five minutes, girls!" Mrs Giles called back.

It was time to set off for the audition!

Chapter 4

When the Glitter Girls arrived at the theatre, they were in for a shock! Mrs Giles had told them that other children from the local drama and ballet schools had been invited to come along to the audition – but they hadn't realized there would be so many of them.

"This is just like the talent competition!" Flo sighed, thinking about the time the Glitter Girls had performed their own ballet. They'd managed to come first!

"It's packed with people. . ." Zoe said, feeling despondent.

"Do you think we stand a chance?" Charly wondered.

"Just as good a chance as everyone else!" Hannah said.

"Yes," said Meg confidently. "Hannah's right! Come on – lets go and sign ourselves in."

Mrs Giles went with the Glitter Girls to the registration desk that had been set up in the foyer of the theatre.

"Right, girls," said the girl on the registration desk. "If you'd like to go through the doors and take a seat in the stalls, Marie, the dance captain, will tell you what to do. . . Now then, who's next?"

"What's a dance captain?" Flo asked as they followed the girl's instructions.

"She's responsible for looking after all the extras who work on the productions," Mrs Giles explained. "She helps the dancers learn their steps and gets them organized for performances. And on top of that she performs as well!"

"Cool!" said Zoe.

"She sounds really important," Charly said, as

she scanned the auditorium, looking for the girl most likely to be Marie.

"Hey, that must be her there," said Hannah, pointing to a tall girl with long dark hair who was standing chatting to some of the others who had already taken their place in the stalls.

"That's right!" Mrs Giles laughed.

"Morning!" Marie beamed at the Glitter Girls as they sat down. "Can you pin this number to your T-shirts, please? On the front, so that the director can read it. Thanks. Hey – great jackets!"

"Thanks," said Meg, taking the numbers and distributing them amongst her friends.

"Oh no – 56! That's high," Hannah sighed as she pinned her number on.

"There are a lot of people here, aren't there?" sighed Flo.

"Never mind," Zoe comforted them. "We're going to do our best – that's all we can do!"

"That's right," Mrs Giles said. "Listen, is it OK if I disappear? The audition is due to start soon

31

and I promised to go and sort some things out in Wardrobe. I'll come and find you later."

"Sure," Hannah said.

"Good luck, girls!" Mrs Giles smiled, holding up her crossed fingers in front of her. "I'll be rooting for you!"

The Glitter Girls sat looking around them as more children turned up to take their seats and be given numbers.

"There must be over seventy of us now," said Meg.

"Hey, look!" Charly pointed. "There are some girls from school!"

The Glitter Girls waved, pleased to see some faces they knew in the crowd.

Just then, two women and a man appeared near the stage. All the children in the theatre fell silent as they watched them chatting and then walking down the aisle to take their seats behind a big table that was at the back of the theatre, in the stalls.

"Do you think one of them's the director?" Meg hissed.

"Should think so," Hannah confirmed.

"Right then, time to start, everyone!" Marie smiled. The audition had begun!

★ ♥ ★ ♥ ★ ♥ ★

Although they were nervous, the Glitter Girls began to have a great time as the audition got going. After Viva, the pantomime director, had introduced herself, Zack the choreographer and Frankie the musical director, she got everyone busy with lots of warm-up routines. First they did some singing exercises.

"These are to warm up your vocal chords!" explained Frankie, the woman who was in charge of the music.

"This is fun!" Charly said, smiling broadly as the Glitter Girls joined everyone else in singing scales. They were told to sing silly things like "ha ha ha, ha ha ha" and "moo moo moo" to a piano accompaniment as part of the vocal exercises.

Then they got to do some simple dance steps with Marie to warm up their muscles before they were asked to perform their audition piece.

"OK," Viva said. "Let's get going. I'll take you first – er – you there!" She pointed to Hannah. "Number 56, the one with the lovely red hair. Everyone else take your seats please until you are called to come on stage."

Hannah was frozen to the spot with surprise for a moment or two. She couldn't believe she'd been called out at the beginning. She'd just assumed they'd start with number one! Hannah gulped and closed her eyes for a second, trying to clear her head of any nerves. Then she opened them again and said, "But I need to be with the rest of the Glitter Girls! We've done our routine together!"

"Sorry? Glitter Girls?" the director said, looking confused.

It was Meg who explained about their song and dance routine, and then Viva laughed and said, "OK girls – Glitter Girls! On stage, please – quickly! We've got lots of people to get through this morning."

"Here's our backing track." Meg handed over a CD to Marie.

"Thanks," Marie said. "Which track?"

"Number five," Hannah said quickly as the girls scrambled up the steps and on to the stage.

The Glitter Girls were nervous. But they took their positions and Hannah counted them in.

"Five, six, seven, eight!"

Everything was going well and the Glitter Girls were twirling confidently around the stage when they were suddenly stopped.

"Thanks! Take a seat!" the director called out. "Next! Hurry now!"

The Glitter Girls looked at each other in horror. They had only got halfway through. They couldn't have been that bad, could they?

Chapter 5

Marie ushered the Glitter Girls quickly off the stage and pushed them back towards their seats.

"What went wrong?" Meg whispered to Hannah as the next girl took her place on the stage.

"I don't know!" she whispered back.

Almost tearfully, the Glitter Girls watched the girl's performance. But, just like them, she was stopped before she got to the end. What was going on? The same thing happened to the next boy – and everyone who went after that. All at once, the Glitter Girls realized that it hadn't been something that they had done wrong when they did their set. They'd obviously been stopped because there was just so much to get through!

"Phew!" Flo whispered dramatically when the last duo climbed down from the stage.

There was silence in the auditorium as the musical director, choreographer and director huddled together. Then they handed a slip of paper to Marie and left the auditorium.

"OK, boys and girls," Marie smiled. "Viva wants to thank you all for coming here today and says you've all done a great job. Now, we only need ten of you for the pantomime and we've got to whittle our numbers down a bit for the next stage. Can the following numbers please stay?"

Marie began reading out a list of numbers.

The Glitter Girls looked at each other anxiously. Meg felt sick – supposing only some of them were chosen? Supposing she was the only one of the Glitter Girls who wasn't! Meg was panicking so much that she didn't even hear what Marie was saying. She was woken from her thoughts by Flo.

"Isn't it great!"

"What?" Meg said.

"Weren't you listening, Meg?" Hannah asked. "We've been called out to stay for the next bit!"

"All five of us!" Zoe gasped excitedly.

"Phew!" Meg sighed, her panic over.

"What do you think will happen next?" Charly wanted to know.

"Do you think we'll have to do our routine again?" Flo asked.

But before anyone could answer, Marie asked all the children who'd been chosen to stay to come up on stage again.

"OK," she explained, handing out a sheet of paper. "Have a read through these words to yourselves. The next thing we want you to do is to read it out at the front of the stage."

"On our own?" one of the boys standing at the back asked.

"Yes – as clearly and as loudly as you can without shouting," Marie replied.

So the next bit of the audition began. Everyone was nervous and some of the children had to start twice – including Flo. When everyone had done their bit, they all stood silently on stage while Viva and the others huddled together talking.

Eventually, Viva came up on to the stage.

"Wow," she said. "What a talented bunch you are today. Now, I'm afraid it's time to get the numbers down again."

All of the children looked round at each other. The Glitter Girls gulped. Would it be now that all or some of them had to go home?

Viva started to read out the numbers.

"Thanks again to you all for coming today – now we want these people to stay for the next round of the audition. . ."

Meg wasn't the only Glitter Girl to have butterflies in her tummy!

The numbers were announced . . . all the Glitter Girls were still in!

★ ♥ ★ ♥ ★ ♥ ★

After a short break, during which they had the chance to grab a refreshing drink, the Glitter Girls were called back with everyone else to sing a song.

"This is hard work!" Flo whispered to Hannah.

"I know," she replied. "And there's only fifteen of us left!"

"Marie was in the loo when I went in there," Charly hissed. "She says we're going to do something with the choreographer. He's the one called Zack."

But there was no more time to chat as Marie approached and said, "Right! Let's dance!"

Zack, with the help of Marie, took the remaining boys and girls through a dance routine. Marie did it once in front of them and then they were asked to run through it behind her, facing

Viva, Frankie the musical director and Zack, who had taken his seat back with the other two.

"OK, everyone? Five, six, seven, eight!"

When it was over, everyone sat down on the stage while the three people behind the table huddled together talking.

"What do you think, Hannah?" Meg whispered to her friend.

"I don't know," she replied honestly. "We did our best – but were we good enough?"

All five of the Glitter Girls hoped so!

After a few more minutes though, the director bounced up on to the stage and thanked them all for coming.

"It's been a tough decision – you are all so talented I wish I could use you all. But sadly I can't. Can I ask the following people to stay behind: 76, 4, 32, 11, 65. . ."

The Glitter Girls looked at each other in horror! She only needed ten people and she'd already called out five numbers!

". . .56. . ."

Hannah!

". . .58. . ."

Meg!

". . .55. . ."

Charly! Would Flo and Zoe be with their best friends too?

". . .54. . ."

Zoe! Flo's heart sank. She couldn't bear it if she got left out of the pantomime.

". . .and 57! Well done, everybody!"

Flo was in! All of them were in! They were going to be in the Christmas pantomime!

"Go Glitter!" the girls screamed, hugging each other excitedly!

★ ♥ ★ ♥ ★ ♥ ★

The following afternoon, the Glitter Girls met up in Zoe's bedroom for a meeting.

"It's so fantastic!" Flo said, hugging her knees. "I was so worried that we might not all get in!"

"It's going to be great," agreed Meg. "And this list of rehearsals isn't too bad, is it?"

Fortunately, most of the rehearsals were on Saturday mornings so it meant that the Glitter Girls wouldn't have to miss many of their usual after-school things like ballet, swimming and riding lessons.

"Do you think your mum knows what our costumes are going to be like?" Zoe asked Hannah.

"Actually, I asked Mum last night," Hannah explained. "She says we're going to have a furry mask and a kind of all-over leotard thing – I think she called it a unitard."

"I'm sure they'll be brilliant if your mum's got anything to do with it," Flo said, smiling.

"I really want to meet Cat Deeley!" Charly said. "Do you think she'll be able to give me some tips on how to make it as a television presenter?"

"I wonder how much we'll see the stars?" Zoe said.

"Yes – do you think Ant and Dec will remember us from ChariTV?" Hannah asked.

The Glitter Girls had met Ant and Dec when they had taken part in a telethon on behalf of their school earlier in the year. It had been a great day. Ant and Dec had been really funny and had helped the Glitter Girls to collect loads of autographs.

"Maybe. . ." said Meg, pulling her notebook out of her jacket pocket. "Listen, we've got loads to do this Christmas – with the bazaar as well as the pantomime. We're going to have to be even more organized than usual."

The four other Glitter Girls exploded with laughter.

"With you to help us," Zoe giggled, "we're bound to be all right!"

"What's the first thing we've got to do then?" Flo asked.

Meg checked the list they had been given by Marie.

"A costume-fitting with Hannah's mum!"

"Go Glitter!" the others replied.

Chapter 6

The following Wednesday afternoon the Glitter Girls went along to Hannah's house after school for their first costume fittings.

"Lucky we know you, Mrs Giles – otherwise we'd have needed to go to the theatre to do this, wouldn't we?" Flo said, as she and her friends made themselves at home in Hannah's mum's workroom.

"It shouldn't take long today, anyway," Mrs Giles said, pulling a notebook across the top of her work bench. "I've still got your measurements from when you did the talent show. I just want to make sure you haven't grown too much!"

"Can I go first? Please!" Charly begged.

"Well, I don't see why not," Mrs Giles laughed. "Arms up, then."

After a short while, all five girls had been measured and Mrs Giles compared the last fitting she had done.

"Just a few tweaks here and there," she confirmed. "Now – do you want to see the designs?"

"Yes!" the Glitter Girls cried.

Mrs Giles picked up a large envelope from the tabletop and pulled out two drawings. They looked just like the ones that the Glitter Girls had done when they entered the Girl's Dream fashion show competition. There were samples of fabric pinned to the drawings and lots of notes written all over them. Mrs Giles spread out the drawings on her work bench.

"Wow!" said Zoe.

"So cute!" exclaimed Hannah.

In front of the Glitter Girls were two drawings of a gorgeous little mouse complete with whiskers, a long tail and twinkling eyes.

"Is this furry fabric what the costumes will be made of?" Meg asked, stroking the swatch of fabric pinned next to one of the pictures.

"Yes," said Mrs Giles. "It's really soft, isn't it?"

"Is there a hole in the back of the costume for us to climb into?" Zoe wondered.

"Sort of," Mrs Giles explained. "And the face is a mask that you put on."

"But with these little black eyes, how can we see?" Flo asked.

"Well, on the actual mask there will be two holes cut underneath the little black eyes," Mrs Giles explained. "And you will be able to see out of those."

"Cool," said Hannah.

"I just love the whiskers and the tail!" Zoe chuckled.

"So do you think you will like your costumes?" Mrs Giles wanted to know.

"Go Glitter!" the girls shouted in agreement.

★ ♥ ★ ♥ ★ ♥ ★

For the next two weeks, the Glitter Girls were busier than ever! On Saturday mornings, they all went along to the local theatre to meet up with Zack, the pantomime's choreographer who had been at their audition.

"We've got to learn a couple of dances," Zack had explained at their first rehearsal. "Then, once you've learnt them, bits of them will be used throughout the show every time you come on stage."

"You mean we've got a kind of theme music and dance?" Hannah asked.

"That's it exactly!" Zack smiled. "And once you've mastered the steps you'll be learning an accompanying song with Frankie, the musical director."

"Cool," said Meg.

"Right then, Marie and I will start and you see if you can follow us," Zack said.

The pianist, who was sitting in the corner of the orchestra pit, began to play, and Zack and Marie spun their way across the stage in front of everyone.

At first, all of the children found it difficult to get the whole routine right. It was Hannah who picked it up first.

"That's it!" Zack called in delight when he saw Hannah. "Come up in front and do it with me."

Hannah was thrilled to be asked to demonstrate with Zack and Marie! And with the three of them dancing together it wasn't long before the others got the hang of it as well.

On the second Saturday, Frankie joined Zack in taking the rehearsal and soon enough the ten mice were singing along to the music.

"You see – I knew we'd picked the right children to help us!" Frankie beamed in delight. "Let's do it one more time! Five, six, seven, eight. . ."

Everyone was exhausted but extremely happy when the rehearsal drew to a close at lunchtime.

"See you all next week!" Frankie called to them as they were leaving the auditorium.

★　♥　★　♥　★　♥　★

On the Sunday afternoon, the Glitter Girls met up at Charly's house. It was the afternoon that they had put aside to help Charly's mum and dad wrap the presents for the Christmas Bazaar.

"Thanks so much for coming over to help, girls," Mrs Fisher said, gesturing to the Glitter Girls that they should take a seat at the kitchen table.

The table was already laden with things. In the middle were two piles of presents: dolls, trains, cars, puzzles – all sorts of toys. There was also a pile of wrapping paper, already cut into large squares, and three big rolls of sticky tape.

"So what do we have to do?" Meg said, keen to get started.

"Well, this pile of presents is for boys," Mrs Fisher began to explain. "And this one is for girls."

"But once they are wrapped, how are we going to know whether they are a boy's present or a girl's present?" Zoe questioned.

"Simple," said Charly. "Boys' presents need to be wrapped in this paper." She pointed to the rolls of shiny red paper.

"And girls' in this!" Flo said, holding up a different design.

"Exactly," Mrs Fisher smiled. "Ready, girls?"

"Go Glitter!" they cried, and the Glitter Girls got busy.

As they wrapped, the Glitter Girls started to sing their pantomime songs. It made the wrapping go quicker – but all of them found it hard not to leap up and start dancing as well.

"There's no time for that!" Mrs Fisher joked.

An hour later, Flo sealed up the last present and dropped it into the girls' box. "Finished!"

"Sorry, but we haven't!" Mrs Fisher smiled at the Glitter Girls as she stood up.

"But there aren't any more presents!" Meg declared.

"Oh – you've finished wrapping the presents for the older boys and girls," Charly's mum agreed. "But we've still got all the presents for the younger children to wrap yet! They can all be wrapped in this third lot of paper."

"Let's get going, then!" Meg said, cheering everyone else on."

It was some time later that the Glitter Girls finished and Mrs Fisher asked, "Who's for some chocolate cake and a glass of milk?"

"Me!" all five Glitter Girls said at once.

★ ♥ ★ ♥ ★ ♥ ★

Two pieces of chocolate cake later, Flo said, "Well, that was a lot of presents, wasn't it?"

"Certainly was," Charly agreed.

"So, since we're thinking about the bazaar – what do we need to wear?" Hannah asked.

"Your mum's helping with that," Mrs Fisher explained, looking at Hannah. "Luckily, there are some costumes left over from last year's pantomime at the theatre and Mrs Giles thinks that they should fit you with a few alterations."

"Wicked!" Zoe said.

"When do we get to try them out?" Meg wanted to know.

"Probably one day after school next week," Mrs Fisher said.

"Christmas pixies one day and mice the next!" Hannah exclaimed.

"We'd better make sure that we don't get them mixed up and wear the wrong thing on the wrong day!" Meg cried – and everyone laughed.

 **Chapter 7**

On Monday afternoon after school, the Glitter Girls met up at Charly's house.

"So what else do we need to do for the bazaar?" Meg asked.

"Not much," Charly replied. "Mum says that most of the work we've got to do will be on the day of the bazaar itself. She's got some mums and dads helping to decorate Santa's Grotto."

"So we've just got to turn up on the day and help Santa then?" Flo queried.

"Yes," said Charly.

"Cool!" said Zoe.

"Well, that gives us lots of time to concentrate on the pantomime," Hannah said.

"Definitely," Meg agreed. "We've got an extra

rehearsal with Zack and Frankie on Friday after school, haven't we?"

"It's only three weeks before the pantomime opens," Flo said.

"I can't wait for it to begin!" Hannah hugged her knees towards her as she snuggled down in a beanbag in Charly's bedroom. "But do you think we'll be ready in time?"

"We've got to be," Meg said.

"I hope so," Flo said. "I mean, we've learnt our parts and it's not that long before we really do go on stage!"

"I asked Mum if she thought we might meet some of the stars and she said that they were popping into the theatre for their rehearsals a lot now – so maybe we will get to see them soon!" Hannah said.

★ ♥ ★ ♥ ★ ♥ ★

It was a busy week at school with everyone having to practise the carols and songs that were going to be performed at the end of term concert. Some of the children had been asked to read poems and stories as well. It was one time when the Glitter Girls were pleased that none of them had been asked to take a solo part!

On the Friday afternoon, Zoe's mum took the Glitter Girls straight from school to the rehearsal at the theatre.

"I thought you might be hungry," said Dr Baker, handing round packets of sandwiches.

"Thanks, Dr Baker," said Hannah and Meg.

"Thanks, Mum – I'm starving," mumbled Zoe, in between mouthfuls.

"Me too!" agreed Flo.

When they got to the theatre, Frankie and Zack were waiting in the auditorium, keen to start the rehearsal as soon as possible.

"Oh good!" Zack smiled. "Only two more people to come now. We've got to run through all your sets, ready for the rehearsal with Viva tomorrow!"

Quickly, the Glitter Girls changed out of their school uniforms and into their tracksuit bottoms and T-shirts, ready for action. By the time they got back to the auditorium, the final boy extras had arrived and they were ready to start the rehearsal.

"Hi, everyone!" Zack smiled. "Let's do a quick warm-up with Marie and then we'll begin."

★ ♥ ★ ♥ ★ ♥ ★

The piano rang out and Marie winked at her mice – the warm-up was over and the rehearsal was about to start.

"Five, six, seven, eight!" Zack called and the ten mice found themselves tapping their feet to the rhythm, ever keen to start their routine. It was a mixture of ballet and jazz steps. They took their positions. . .

"That was excellent, everyone!" Frankie called, as the last notes of the music died away.

"Yes – very good," Zack agreed enthusiastically.

"Shall we take a short breather before we go into the next number?"

"Please!" the mice all called at once.

Carefully, the Glitter Girls and the other children all climbed down the steps that led from the stage to the seats, all keen to grab a drink.

"I'm dreading the next bit!" Meg confided to her friends. "I'm bound to forget the words."

"You?" Hannah exclaimed.

"But you're so organized," Zoe said. "You learnt the words before any of us!"

As the butterflies fluttered in Meg's tummy, Zack called them back on stage, this time to do the routine when they all got to sing a line on their own. As before, everything started according to plan and, as the mice sang and danced, Frankie and Zack called out encouragement.

It was in the third verse that the mice sang their solos and Charly and Hannah slid smoothly through theirs, not long after followed by Flo and Zoe. Meg was the second to last one to sing her solo and her four best friends skipped and danced their way around the stage, eagerly looking forward to hearing her sing.

They were all delighted when Meg sang her line and, soon after, the number ended.

"See!" Zoe whispered comfortingly to her friend, "I knew you wouldn't forget!"

"That was just excellent, boys and girls!" Frankie said.

"Yes – I think Viva is going to be very pleased with you all tomorrow," Zack said. "Remember – ten o'clock sharp for rehearsal!"

★ ♥ ★ ♥ ★ ♥ ★

The Glitter Girls were beside themselves with excitement when they met at Hannah's house the next morning. They couldn't wait to get to the theatre so that they could try on their costumes and perform in front of the director!

60

Marie spotted the Glitter Girls as soon as they arrived at the theatre.

"Hi, girls," she beamed at them. "I'll take you to the official dressing rooms. Follow me!"

A trail of would-be mice eagerly followed Marie through a door just to one side of the stage and along a series of corridors.

"I don't suppose I'll ever remember my way back!" Charly whispered to her friends.

"Right," Marie said, opening a large door labelled *Dressing Room* 6. "Boys this side," she said, pointing behind a sort of screen that divided the room into two, "girls this one! I expect you're keen to see your costumes now!"

With a flourish, Marie pulled a cover from a big rack on one side of the dressing room to reveal ten gorgeous, fluffy mice costumes! Attached to each hanger, there was also a mask and a pair of black ballet shoes.

"Wow!" all ten children exclaimed at once.

Marie laughed, pleased that her group of dancers were so thrilled with their costumes.

"Each costume has been labelled," Marie explained. "So find yours and get changed. Just make sure you don't drag the costumes on the floor."

"Or my mum will go mad!" Hannah exclaimed, and everyone else laughed.

"These are just brilliant!" Zoe said.

"They are so lifelike!" cried Flo.

"Squeak, squeak!" said Meg, who was the first to get into her costume.

"Eek!" Marie screamed, pretending to be scared and jumping up on to a chair. "There are ten giant mice in the room!"

Chapter 8

The Glitter Girls and their other mousey companions couldn't resist practising their steps as they followed Marie back into the auditorium ready to start their rehearsal with Viva.

Just like the other rehearsals, the Glitter Girls went straight into the auditorium but unlike the other days, there were more musicians in the orchestra pit than just the pianist. There were also more people milling around the place and various people on stage.

Hannah's mum was waiting eagerly to greet them as they came in.

"How do they feel?" she asked, walking along to inspect the line of mice – lifting their arms and adjusting their tails.

"Brilliant!" one of the boys said from behind his mask.

"We feel just like the real thing!" squeaked Zoe.

"I think I may have to make a few changes," Mrs Giles said, pulling up one mouse's leg which was a bit too baggy.

"There's no time for that now," Marie said, nodding her head over Mrs Giles's shoulder. "Here comes Viva!"

"Good morning, everyone! Lovely to see you all again! Don't you look fantastic!"

"Good morning!" all the mice replied.

"I've been hearing how well you've all been doing with Marie, Zack and Frankie. We've got a lot to get through this morning so can I see your first number, please?"

Swiftly, Marie ushered her mice up on to the stage. The orchestra struck its first chord. The dress rehearsal had begun!

★ ♥ ★ ♥ ★ ♥ ★

The Glitter Girls, along with the other mice, were having such a great time that they raced through the first number and their various links, just as Frankie and Zack had taught them. Viva seemed really pleased with them.

"You can take a break now, boys and girls, while we just rehearse some other bits," Viva said.

Grateful for their chance to rest, the ten mice, followed by Marie, made their way to sit in the stalls, making sure that they didn't sit on their tails.

"It's a relief to take this mask off!" Meg whispered. "It's difficult to see what's going on some of the time."

"You should speak to Mum about it," Hannah suggested.

But before Meg could reply, Charly grabbed her arm and said: "Wow! Look – there's Cat Deeley!"

"Where?" the other Glitter Girls replied, just

loud enough for the other mice to hear and look up as well.

"There!" Charly pointed.

Sure enough, there on stage was Cat – rehearsing with Ant and Dec!

"Oh!" gulped Zoe. "She's so pretty!"

"Wow!" exclaimed Flo.

Then silence fell and everyone watched entranced as the three stars sang and danced together. Ant and Dec were so funny as the Ugly Sisters that the Glitter Girls couldn't help laughing really loudly.

"Shush!" Marie winked. "You don't want us to get in trouble!

After that, the Glitter Girls and the other mice made sure that they kept their hands over their mouths so as not to laugh too loudly.

★ ♥ ★ ♥ ★ ♥ ★

A while later, Viva called all of the mice back on stage, ready for them to rehearse their next number with Cat Deeley. All through their other rehearsals, they had practised with Marie pretending to be Cat but now they would be performing with the real star. Marie had changed and was also in costume.

"Hi!" Cat said cheerily, smiling at them all.

They were all so excited and nervous about meeting her that the Glitter Girls only managed to squeak a "hello" in response.

"I can see you make really good mice!" Cat laughed.

The number that they were about to sing was the one with all the solo lines. They'd rehearsed it until they were perfect. Meg was due to sing last.

"Please, Cinderella, don't you fret!" sang the mouse before her.

The band played their musical response and then it was Meg's turn to sing "Your prince must be on his way yet!"

But instead of Meg's lovely voice, there was

nothing – except for the noise of the musicians! And then one of the boy mice tripped over a piece of scenery at the back of the stage. There was a loud crash as it was knocked over!

"Whoa! Hold up!" the director called, and she climbed up from the audience on to the stage. "What went wrong there?"

"Oh no! I'm really sorry," Meg's voice trembled as she spoke.

Her friends stood by helpless, wondering what had gone wrong. Meg was always so good at everything!

"Is there a problem?" Viva asked. "Are you all right in there?"

Frankie helped take her mask off, revealing a flushed and tearful Meg underneath. At the back of the stage, Marie was helping to sort out Billy, the boy who had tripped.

"What happened, Meg?" Frankie asked, sprinting across the stage. "You usually get your lines just right!"

"I – I just don't know," Meg said, holding her head low. "I couldn't really see very well in my mask. I kind of got lost and was concentrating so hard on my steps that I missed the bit where I was meant to sing."

"Is there something wrong with the costume, Meg?" Hannah's mum asked, stepping out from the wings where she had been fixing another actor's costume.

"We've got to get this sorted!" Viva said. "We've only got a couple of weeks to go. . ."

The ten mice, including the five Glitter Girls, stood silently on the stage. Everything had gone so well at all the rehearsals until now. Viva was standing to one side of the stage talking quietly with Zack and Frankie.

"What do you think they're saying?" Meg asked Marie, trying to hold back her tears of disappointment with herself.

"Don't worry," Marie said, gently touching Meg's arm and trying to make her feel better.

"They are probably just arranging another rehearsal."

"It'll be all right," Charly said, smiling.

Viva walked over and called out to everyone, "Can we just run through that whole song again please? I'd like to see if we can get it right this time."

"Back to your positions everyone!" Marie winked at her mice.

The music started again and everyone tried hard to do their best, including Meg – who was desperate to make it work properly this time. But it was almost as if the harder she tried, the worse things got for her. She lost confidence in her singing and was hesitant in her dance steps. Although she'd managed to get through the number Meg knew that she hadn't really done her best.

When the music finished at the end, Viva called out, "Er, thanks everyone. I'm sure it's going to be fine but I think we need to do another run through with everyone in costume. Let's meet back here next Saturday for an extra rehearsal – same time, same place. You'll have your other usual rehearsals with Zack and Frankie as well."

Meg was so relieved! She thought that Viva was going to say that she couldn't be in the pantomime and they'd have to find someone else! Marie ushered everyone back off the stage and to their dressing room.

On the girls' side of the dressing room, the Glitter Girls sat down and looked at each other in silence. It was Meg who spoke first. "I'm so sorry," she said.

"It's OK!" Zoe said as she carefully began to climb out of her costume.

"No, it's not," Flo snapped.

"Flo!" Charly cried. "Meg just made a mistake, that's all. It could have happened to any of us."

"Please, Flo," Meg sighed, holding back her tears.

"But it isn't OK, is it?" Flo said impatiently. "Haven't any of you worked it out?"

"Worked what out?" Hannah asked, looking totally confused.

"Next Saturday," Flo barked. "The extra rehearsal is next Saturday. The same day as the bazaar!"

"Oh no!" Meg cried.

Chapter 9

"What are we going to do?" Charly asked. "We can't be in two places at once!"

"Precisely!" said Flo, glad that someone had finally understood the crisis.

It was the final straw for Meg, who put her hands over her face and sobbed.

"Oh Meg, don't," Hannah said, trying to comfort her friend.

Flo felt bad about saying something. "Meg, I'm sorry. It's not your fault."

"But if I'd got it right we wouldn't be having an extra rehearsal, would we?" Meg sniffed.

"Meg? Girls?" Mrs Giles came into the dressing room. "Is everything all right? Let me see your costume, Meg. I obviously need to adjust your mask."

Meg looked up and said, "No, it was my fault, Mrs Giles – I mucked it up!"

"Actually, Meg," Mrs Giles said, looking up from poking around inside Meg's mouse mask. "I don't think it was just nerves on stage."

"What do you mean?" Hannah said.

"It was my fault, I think. Look," Mrs Giles said apologetically as she pointed to the label inside the mask. "I gave you the wrong mask. This one is for Charly! I must have put the right label inside and then hung it on the wrong costume! I am so sorry, Meg."

"But Charly's mask is OK," Zoe exclaimed.

"Actually," Charly said. "If I'm honest, it was a bit uncomfortable, Mrs Giles."

"I expect it was!" Mrs Giles laughed. "Meg's mask didn't have room for your glasses! And your mask has the eyes set in a different position."

"Which is why Meg couldn't see properly!" Flo cried.

"Here, try these, you two," Mrs Giles said,

swapping the two masks over and handing them to Meg and Charly.

"Hey, I can see!" Meg said.

"And this is much more comfy!" Charly added.

"Sorted then!" Mrs Giles smiled.

"But it isn't!" Flo said, and she explained to Mrs Giles about the extra rehearsal now being at the same time that the Glitter Girls were meant to be at the bazaar.

"Oh, I see," Mrs Giles said slowly.

"It's a disaster!" Charly said. "We can't be in both places. We'll have to let Dad down!"

"No!" the other four cried.

"Hmm," Mrs Giles said. "Let me have a think while I make some adjustments to your costumes. Can you all pop them back on for me to check?"

The Glitter Girls fretted and flustered as Mrs Giles worked with her pins until she was satisfied with how the mice looked.

"Thanks, you lot," she said when she was finished. "Now I need to go and check the boys."

"But what can we do about the bazaar?" Meg wailed.

"When I've finished here," Mrs Giles said, "I think we should all go and see Viva to explain the problem. After all, I'm supposed to be at the bazaar as well, so I can't really be here either, can I?"

"Do you think Viva will understand?" Charly wondered aloud.

"We won't know until we've asked, will we?" Mrs Giles said.

★ ♥ ★ ♥ ★ ♥ ★

The Glitter Girls had to wait quietly at the back of the auditorium while the director rehearsed a big scene with all of the stars of the show.

"Hey, look! There's Pauline from *EastEnders*!"

said Charly, pointing out the actress Wendy Richard.

"And there's that other boy from *EastEnders* too!" said Zoe.

It was fun watching the rehearsal, but all the time Meg and the other Glitter Girls were sitting worrying about the problem they had with the rehearsal and the bazaar. They couldn't let Charly's mum and dad down. But on the other hand, they couldn't let the pantomime down either.

If only I could have got it right! Meg thought.

Eventually, Viva called a break.

"Now's our chance," Mrs Giles said. "Come on."

She walked towards the stage, the Glitter Girls following behind her.

"Viva – have you got a minute?"

"Sorry?" Viva peered down from the brightly lit stage, struggling to see in the darkness of the auditorium.

"Here!" Mrs Giles waved. "We wondered if we could have a word with you?"

"Of course," Viva said, climbing down the steps and past the orchestra pit.

"There's a bit of a problem with the rehearsal next Saturday," explained Mrs Giles.

"Well, we have to have it – after the problems today," Viva said, slightly impatiently. "Everything has to be right on the day and we open in two weeks – less than that, actually!"

Meg, still feeling dreadful about making such a mess of things, felt that she should explain.

"You see, we've promised to help at the town Christmas Bazaar. We're going to be Santa's helpers and we've got costumes and everything ready."

"And this extra rehearsal is at the same time as the bazaar!" Zoe added.

"And we can't be in both places!" Hannah put in.

"We can't let the bazaar down now!" wailed Flo.

"We've promised!" Charly said emphatically.

Viva looked at the Glitter Girls.

"Hmm," she said, scratching her head. "It is a bit of a problem, isn't it. But we really do need to have the rehearsal."

The Glitter Girls said nothing but looked pleadingly at Viva.

"Look," Viva said. "When does this bazaar thing finish?"

"It starts at ten and finishes at two," Meg explained efficiently.

"OK," Viva sighed. "You win! Obviously you must go to the bazaar because you've promised – but!"

"Yes?" the Glitter Girls all said at once.

"We still need to have an extra rehearsal. So we'll have to have it on Saturday afternoon after the bazaar. You girls are just very lucky that there isn't a matinee performance next

Saturday! Just make sure you tell all the other mice!"

"Go Glitter!" they all screamed at once.

★ ♥ ★ ♥ ★ ♥ ★

The following week flew by. It was the last week of term and so there was the school concert as well as a trip that the school made every year to the old people's home in town. Then of course there was the school Christmas party – they had a disco and everyone was allowed to wear their favourite clothes!

After school every day, the Glitter Girls practised their songs and dances for the pantomime. They had the usual rehearsals with Marie, Frankie and Zack at the theatre but they practised at home as well. They were all determined to get it right on the night – especially Meg!

And in between doing things for the pantomime, the Glitter Girls tried on their costumes and helped Charly's mum to make some of the signs telling people where to go to find Santa.

On Friday night, the Glitter Girls met up at Charly's house to organize themselves for the next day.

"It's going to be really busy!" Meg said, flipping open her notebook and checking her list. "So, you've all got your bags ready?"

"Yes!" Charly, Hannah, Flo and Zoe replied.

"And your picnic lunches?"

"I'm doing mine tomorrow morning," Hannah explained.

"Me too!" the others agreed.

"Costumes?"

"Yes!"

"Looks like we're sorted then!"

"I'm too excited to sleep!" Zoe said, smiling and fiddling with her favourite sparkly hairclip.

"Go Glitter!" the others giggled.

Chapter 10

At nine-thirty the next morning, four Glitter Girls dressed in red tights, red ballet shoes, shimmery red and gold tops and gorgeous red velvet capes trimmed with white fluffy feathers, knocked on the door of Charly's house. She opened the door to greet them.

"Come in! You look great!" Charly said, as her four best friends trooped in.

"Hello, girls!" Mrs Fisher said. "You look fantastic! Shall we go?"

"Go Glitter!" screamed Lily, Charly's younger sister, as she raced to greet the Glitter Girls.

"Go Glitter!" they all screamed back.

★ ♥ ★ ♥ ★ ♥ ★

At the Town Hall, people were busy putting the finishing touches to their stalls.

"Doesn't it look Christmassy?" Zoe sighed, looking round at the fairy lights and decorations all over the walls. At one end of the room there was the most magnificent Christmas tree and just the sight of it made the Glitter Girls tummies tingle with excitement at the thought that Christmas was now so near! But it was the sight of Santa's Grotto that really made them stop in their tracks. For there at the other end of the hall was the most wonderful cave, decorated with shimmering fabric and gossamer gold stars! The Glitter Girls raced over to see it.

"It looks like real snow!" Charly said. "Where's Dad? Oops! I mean, Santa!"

"I'll take you through to him," Mrs Fisher smiled. "I'll show you round."

She led them through the grotto and explained where the Glitter Girls should lead the children when they came to visit Santa.

Deep at the back of the grotto, there was Mr Fisher! He was brilliantly disguised as Santa and Hannah's mum was just putting the finishing touches to his beard.

"Don't you all look great!" Mrs Giles said, pleased with the way the costumes had turned out.

"Come on!" said Mrs Fisher, looking at her watch. "We'd better get you ready – it's nearly time!" And the Glitter Girls all went back to the grotto's entrance.

"Excuse me!" said a young man, approaching the grotto. It was the photographer from the local newspaper. "I need a photograph of you with Santa! So where is he?"

"Ho, ho, ho!" boomed Charly's dad and he stepped out from the grotto.

The man snapped away taking photographs of them all together and then he took one of Lily sitting on Santa's knee. She was tugging his beard and trying to pull it off!"

When he was finished, the photographer asked them to spell their names for him.

"A little bird tells me that you girls are in the pantomime this Christmas too!" the photographer said, writing in his notebook. "You're going to be busy, aren't you?"

Just then, a lady rushed over to the grotto.

"There's a massive queue at the door!" she said enthusiastically. "Only five minutes until opening time. Action stations!"

"Sorry!" Meg apologized to the photographer. "We've got to go!"

★ ♥ ★ ♥ ★ ♥ ★

The morning just seemed to whizz by with the Glitter Girls hardly having time to speak to each other. They had a great time, guiding the little children through the enchanted grotto to Santa. The children were so excited about meeting Santa and they all seemed to love their presents.

Meg, though, was anxious to make sure that the Glitter Girls weren't late leaving the bazaar to get to the rehearsal and she kept checking her watch to make sure they were OK.

"Half an hour to go!" she whispered to Flo, who was helping her to give out the presents.

A few minutes later, Meg was giving a present to a little boy when she fumbled and dropped it.

"Ooops!"

"Never mind – it's not broken!" Flo said. But then she saw the worried expression on her friend's face. "You OK, Meg?"

Meg gulped. "I'm just feeling a bit nervous that's all . . . about the rehearsal."

Flo put her arm round Meg. "It'll be fine," she reassured her. "You'll see."

"But we're only having the rehearsal because of me!" Meg whispered as the little boy was escorted out of the grotto by Charly.

"And Billy!" Flo reminded her. "Anyway, we *all* need the rehearsal!"

"Sure," said Meg. "Come on – let's get on with helping Santa!"

★ ♥ ★ ♥ ★ ♥ ★

At the theatre that afternoon, Viva explained that she wanted to run through the whole pantomime from start to finish – just like the real thing.

"So," Viva said. "Can you all warm up and be ready in fifteen minutes?"

Marie took her mice off to run through their exercises. Fifteen minutes later they were back on stage as instructed.

"Break a leg!" Marie winked.

The rehearsal was about to begin.

★ ♥ ★ ♥ ★ ♥ ★

Half an hour later, Viva rushed on the stage.

"OK – stop there! Now what's the problem?"

But this time none of the Glitter Girls or the other mice needed to worry. This time it was Ant and Dec who'd forgotten their lines!

"You see?" Marie whispered. "Everyone makes mistakes – even Ant and Dec!"

Meg felt so much better after that. So much better that she began to enjoy the rehearsal rather than just feeling nervous that she was going to mess up their routine.

As it happened, all their sections went really smoothly, and by the time the rehearsal was nearly over, the Glitter Girls were enjoying themselves so much they didn't want it to stop!

★ ♥ ★ ♥ ★ ♥ ★

Tired and happy, the Glitter Girls finally got home to Flo's that evening and were treated to a fantastic Chinese meal cooked by Flo's dad.

"So the rehearsal went well, did it?" Mr Eng asked.

"It was OK!" Meg said, smiling with pleasure

and remembering how Viva had told them all how great they all were.

"It was more than OK!" Flo said. "It was fantastic!"

"Yes – the pantomime was brilliant and the bazaar was so much fun!" Hannah said, stuffing her face with noodles as she spoke. She was hungry after such a busy day!

In between mouthfuls of food, the Glitter Girls told Mr and Mrs Eng all about the bazaar and the rehearsal.

"We've got a brief rehearsal on Monday and Tuesday," Zoe explained.

"Then the pantomime opens with the matinee on Wednesday!" Charly yawned.

"Sounds to me like you girls should be getting to bed!" Mr Eng said.

And for once, the Glitter Girls agreed!

Chapter 11

Overture and beginners on stage please!

"That's us!" Meg squeaked from her place in the dressing room.

It was Wednesday afternoon and the first performance of the pantomime was about to start!

"Mice, are you ready?" Marie asked her ten furry friends.

"Yes!" they all replied enthusiastically, trying to control their nerves.

"Then let's go!" Marie beamed.

★ ♥ ★ ♥ ★ ♥ ★

Standing quietly in the wings, the Glitter Girls were in their places, listening to the opening music start up. From behind the other side of the curtain, they could hear an excited gasp from the whole audience as the music began and then silence as they eagerly awaited the first performance of *Cinderella*.

Slowly, the curtain began to rise and there on stage was Cat, dressed in her rags, sweeping the floor of the set that looked exactly like the kitchen of a grand house.

"Where's that lazy girl?" demanded the familiar voice of Ant as he walked confidently on to the stage, closely followed by Dec. Their Ugly Sister costumes were amazing.

"Cinders?" Dec yelled.

That was the first cue for the Glitter Girls and the other mice and immediately they sprang from the wings and scurried just like mice across the stage to scare the Ugly Sisters.

"Mice!" the sisters yelled. "Vermin!"

The Glitter Girls' first ever pantomime performance had begun!

★ ♥ ★ ♥ ★ ♥ ★

In the interval, Viva came to visit the mice in their dressing room.

"Well done, everybody!" she said. "You are all doing wonderfully well! It's a great success! Keep it up!"

"Go Glitter!" the five best friends called instinctively.

"Go Glitter!" the other five mice replied.

★ ♥ ★ ♥ ★ ♥ ★

When the second act began, the Glitter Girls were having such a great time that they forgot to feel nervous any more. They sang and danced their hearts out and if they hadn't been so excited they would have almost felt disappointed when the curtain finally closed at the end.

Stepping out to take their bows was magical and the Glitter Girls were just able to make out some of the members of their families who had come to see the performance. It was very tempting to wave, but the girls all knew that wouldn't have been professional and just gave huge, beaming smiles in the right directions instead.

When the applause finally died down and the curtain fell, Wendy Richard – looking splendid in her Fairy Godmother costume – turned to the mice and said, "Well done, you lot! You were fantastic! Did you enjoy it?"

They all nodded their heads in confirmation.

"So you're coming back for the other performances then?"

"Yes!" they all replied.

"Go Glitter!" Wendy said laughing – she'd heard them yell their trademark catchphrase at rehearsals.

"Go Glitter!" the five best friends and the other mice replied in excitement.

★ ♥ ★ ♥ ★ ♥ ★

Back in their dressing room afterwards, the Glitter Girls heard a knock on the door.

"Can we have your autographs, please?"

It was Mr Eng – and he wasn't alone! In fact he was with some of the other Glitter Girls' mums and dads.

"You were all wonderful!" said Dr Baker proudly, giving Zoe a kiss.

"Did you enjoy it?" Meg asked her dad.

"I wouldn't have missed it for the world!" he said. "You were all brilliant!"

"So," said Hannah's dad, "who's for some food?"

"We've booked a table at the restaurant next door – we thought we'd all have a lovely meal to celebrate your opening night, girls!" said Mrs Fisher.

"Wow!" exclaimed Charly. "Could tonight get any better?"

"Yes, so you'd better hurry up and get changed, girls," urged Hannah's dad, "the rest of your families are waiting for the mice stars to make their appearance! I'll wait for you outside."

The girls quickly began to change out of their furry costumes.

"Better not eat too much tonight or we won't be able to fit in our costumes!" said Zoe, laughing.

"Yes," Meg agreed. "And we'd better make sure we get back in time for the next performance!"

"Don't worry," said Mrs Fisher, "we'll get you back here in an hour." She looked round at the girls, who'd changed back into their Glitter Girl jackets and comfy tracksuit bottoms. "Right then," she said. "Let's go!"

★ ♥ ★ ♥ ★ ♥ ★

"Come on mice!" Marie called as the Glitter Girls piled back into the dressing room later that evening. "We've got half an hour – we need to warm up and get back in costume!"

Everyone did as instructed and it didn't seem anything like as long as thirty minutes before they heard another announcement on the theatre tannoy: *Overture and beginners on stage please!*

Already the second performance of *Cinderella* was about to begin and the mice followed Marie to the stage. The Glitter Girls were still buzzing from the lovely meal they'd shared with their families and they felt even more butterflies of excitement as the familiar pantomime music began. In the hidden safety of their positions in the wings, the Glitter Girls hugged each other with excitement.

"Isn't this just the best Christmas ever?" Meg whispered.

"Go Glitter!" her best friends whispered back.